ROCKY & BULLWINKLE

Fearless Firemoose!

By David Corwyn
Illustrated by Hawley Pratt and Harry Garo

 A GOLDEN BOOK • NEW YORK

randomhouse.com/kids

Educators and librarians, for a variety of teaching tools, visit us at RHTeachersLibrarians.com

ISBN 978-0-385-37152-0

Printed in the United States of America

10 9 8 7 6 5 4 3

Random House Children's Books supports the First Amendment and celebrates the right to read.

Once there was a moose. He had **big funny feet.**
He had a great **big funny nose.** And his name was
Bullwinkle J. Moose.

    He liked cupcakes and mooseberry juice. He had them three times
a day—for breakfast, lunch, and dinner. And all day long, Bullwinkle
dreamed that he was a **fearless firemoose.**

In his daydream, he climbed up to a burning roof.
Smoke and cinders swirled all around him.

"Never fear," Bullwinkle said to a little old lady. "Together we will jump safely to the safety net."

So, in his daydream, Bullwinkle jumped. . . .

Babbump! He fell off his chair.

His friends Rocky and Mr. Peabody came rushing in.

"Ohhhh," Bullwinkle groaned. "What's the use? I'll never be a firemoose."

"I know what I would do if I were you," said Mr. Peabody, who was a very clever dog.

"What?" Bullwinkle asked.

"I'd take a train and travel to the city," Mr. Peabody said.

"And I'd go from firehouse to firehouse until I got a job."

What a great idea! Bullwinkle gave a long, happy—

HONNNNNNNK!

Rocky and Mr. Peabody held their ears.

The moose's honk was louder than a thunderclap. It could be heard miles away.

"Hooray!" Bullwinkle cried. "I'm going to the city!"

"All aboooard!" the conductor called at the railroad station. "And no sticking antlers out of windows!"

With a *click* and a *clack* and a *clickety-clack*, the train began to move.

Bullwinkle was on his way!

The clicking song the train made soon put the moose to sleep. And while he slept, he had a dream.

In the dream, Bullwinkle was putting out a fire with a fire hose. Water was gushing from the hose in a steady stream, when suddenly—

Bullwinkle was drenched with water!

"Excuse me," a little boy said. "I spilled some water."

"That's okay," Bullwinkle replied. "I was hoping to make a splash."

Just then, with a bump and a thump, the train stopped.

The conductor said in a worried voice, "There's a herd of cows on the track. And our whistle isn't working. Without a whistle, we can't make the cattle move."

"Stop worrying," Bullwinkle said. "My honk is louder than a thunderclap. It can be heard miles and miles away."

So Bullwinkle went to the front of the train. And he honked.
HONNNNNNNK!
The cows had never heard such a honk before. They bawled
with fright and ran away. And the train could go again.

When the train arrived in the city, Bullwinkle got off.
The conductor called, "Thanks, Bullwinkle!"
Just then, a siren sounded.

Whooooo!

It was a gleaming red fire engine, returning from a fire.

With its siren wailing, the fire engine whizzed through the crowded city streets.

"Wait for me!" Bullwinkle shouted as he ran after it.

The fire engine reached the firehouse. And so did Bullwinkle, gasping for breath.

"Sir," he panted to the chief. "I'd like a job."

First the chief stared. Next he scratched his head. Then he began to snicker. And then he laughed with all his might.

"Don't be a silly goose," laughed the chief. "Who ever heard of a *firemoose?*"

Bullwinkle went from firehouse to firehouse. But all the chiefs just laughed at him.

"It's no use," he groaned. "I'll never be a firemoose."

Just then, the alarm inside a firehouse began to ring!

CLANG! CLANG! CLANG! CLANG! CLANG! CLANG!

STATION NO5

Bullwinkle watched the firemen slide down the pole.
He stared as they jumped onto the side of their fire engine.
And he waited for the siren to go **Whooooo!**
But he never heard it!

The chief said in a worried voice, "The siren is broken. Nobody will hear us coming. And they won't get out of the way."

All the firemen wondered what could be done.

"Never fear!" Bullwinkle shouted. "Bullwinkle is here!"

Bullwinkle sat up front. He honked. And he **HONKED!**
Nobody had ever heard such a honk before. The fire engine
whizzed through the streets. And it reached the fire just in time.

"Thanks," the chief said, shaking hands with Bullwinkle. "We
never would have been in time to put the fire out if not for you.
Take this helmet for your very own. For now you have a job."

What a job it was!
Smoke and cinders...

Up on **burning roofs...**

Steady streams of
gushing water...

Bullwinkle saved **seventy-seven** little old ladies by jumping with them safely down to safety nets. And he won a medal!

Now Bullwinkle is back home again. He still likes cupcakes and mooseberry juice. And still he has them for breakfast, lunch, and dinner.

But he no longer dreams all day long. With his helmet and his medal—Bullwinkle knows he is a *fearless firemoose!*